WOLVES NOT will ̌ BE WOLVES

For all the Little Reds. – F.S.

For Luís and João, thank you for everything. – H.A.

A STUDIO PRESS BOOK

First published in the UK in 2024 by Studio Press,
an imprint of Bonnier Books UK,
4th Floor, Victoria House, Bloomsbury Square, London WC1B 4DA
Owned by Bonnier Books,
Sveavägen 56, Stockholm, Sweden

www.bonnierbooks.co.uk

Text copyright © Frances Stickley 2024
Artwork copyright © Hannah Abbo 2024

1 3 5 7 9 10 8 6 4 2

Hardback ISBN: 978-1-80078-918-0
Paperback ISBN: 978-1-80078-486-4

FSC
www.fsc.org
MIX
Paper | Supporting
responsible forestry
FSC® C104723

Edited by Frankie Jones
Cover designed by Maddox Philpot
Designed by Claire Munday
Production by Nick Read

A CIP catalogue record for this book is available from the British Library
Printed and bound in China

WOLVES NOT WILL BE WOLVES

FRANCES STICKLEY

HANNAH ABBO

STUDIO
PRESS

Little Red was not about to waste another minute.
The big wide world was waiting and she wanted to be in it.

She raced to pack her rucksack,
she rushed towards the gate,

But as she read the King's Decree that warned her to Be Good...

... a gloom of doom and danger seemed to settle on the woods. And suddenly, the journey to her Grandma's house seemed fraught with Big Bads in the woods and all the rules that she'd been taught.

Don't stay out after dark

Don't talk to wolves

At first, Red followed all the Dos and Don'ts the King's men told her,
but as she wandered from the path, she suddenly grew bolder
and stepped into the shadows as she left the path behind her,
until she heard a voice ring with a cautionary reminder...

Do stick to
the path

"Beware, BEWARE!" cried Goldilocks. "The wolf is out today!
You must stick to the path, or you'll be surely snatched away.
He's waiting in the deep, dark woods.

Quick, go on home and hide!"

And she raced towards the nearest house and locked herself inside.

But Red couldn't help but grumble,
"What a silly rule," she sighed,
"when the wolf can wander anywhere,
why should I stay inside?"

Little Red walked on along the path that led towards the glen,
but it wasn't very long before the warning came again.

"BEWARE!" called out the children. "There's a wolf within the woods!
So be sure to hide your eyes or stay disguised inside your hood.

He's a fierce and beastly beasty.
We'll be gobbled up for sure!"

And they ran towards the nearest house
and knocked, twice, on the door.

But Red couldn't help but grumble,
"What a silly rule," she cried,
"when the wolf is still the
Big, Bad Wolf no matter if I hide."

She stumbled on a flower-patch that bloomed between the trees,
and she thought she heard the sound of trot-trot trotting on the breeze.

"BEWARE!" a little pig cried. "There's a big, bad wolf about.
If you stop to pick the flowers, he'll be sure to sniff you out!"

He's a **menace.**

"... So I've heard," Red sighed,
but a feeling, like a fireball, was boiling up inside
and although the pigs cried, "Run and hide!"
she felt her blood run hot...

... and that fiery ball of anger kept her rooted to the spot.

"I could run," Red said, unflinching, "if it means I won't be caught.
I could follow all the RULES TO BEAT THE WOLVES that I've been taught,
but that doesn't solve the problem of the Big, Bad Wolf," she said...

"... There's no one who can change the wolf's behaviour but himself.

But every Don't, and Shan't and Can't and every fearful thought,
it only means we'd blame ourselves if ever we got caught."

"The Big Bads have been stalking
in this forest for too long.

Alone, we might be helpless
but together, we are strong.

So no more hiding in our homes
or hiding in our hoods.

We're taking back our freedom..."

We're taking back our cottages, our forests and our flowers.

We're taking back our Kingdoms...
... and our castles...
... and our towers.

It's time to take the

RULES TO BEAT THE WOLVES

down from the shelf..."

"Together, as we grow, we'll change their minds…
… We'll change the laws."

The woods were full of hollering and cheers from everyone
as they crept out from their hidey-holes and stepped towards the sun,
and as she blinked into the light that glittered through the trees,
Young Red was so excited to run wild...

... and to feel free.

The big, wide world was waiting – how she wanted to be in it!
And Little Red was not about to waste another minute.

Sharing this book with children

A note from Laura Coryton

This book can inspire young readers to speak up when something is unfair, in order to create a more equal society. In doing so, it may also spark difficult and important questions.

For example, Little Red's passion to change the oppressive rules which maintained the tyranny of the Big Bad Wolf may cause children to question the merits of the rules which govern them, too.

To discuss the difference young readers can make, it's important to separate rules from laws. Pieces of legislation – or laws – protected by parliament, require considerable thought and effort to challenge respectfully and successfully. Therefore, it might be helpful to encourage young changemakers to consider the validity of the rules which govern them before they go on to examine the fairness of the national legal system. Local change can be just as powerful as amending a national law, if not more so!

Children can do so by asking themselves the following:

1
Does this rule exist for a good reason?

2
Is there a better way for the rule to achieve its aim? Is there a way it can include more people or perspectives?

3
What alternatives can you think of to this rule? Is your solution respectful and thoughtful?

This process will help build confidence, independence and problem solving skills so they can become the Little Reds of tomorrow, ready to make the world a better place!

Children may also question the wider themes this book examines such as sexism, victim blaming and holding perpetrators of violence to account.

To help children make sense of these big societal issues without feeling overwhelmed, several empowering and positive points can be emphasised by parents and caregivers, including:

If you're ever unsure about something or if you feel something isn't right, always speak to a trusted adult – they are here to help you.

Humans aren't perfect. Since the beginning of time, leaders and lawmakers have made bad decisions and mistakes, which we can experience the impact of today. It's up to brave people like you to help right these wrongs!

Finally, for me, the most important message of this book is that no matter how big a problem may seem, everything is solvable. So long as you stay committed to making the world a better, more equal place, you can truly do anything you set your mind to.

Laura Coryton started the international campaign against Tampon Tax which gained over 300,000 signatures and the backing of many prominent figures including President Obama. She successfully lobbied the UK Government into donating £90m to female-focused charities and to ending the tax in 2021. She's also an author and managing director of social enterprise Sex Ed Matters.